The World of
Emily Windsnap

Emily's Big Discovery

The World of Emily Windsnap

Emily's Big Discovery

Liz Kessler

illustrated by Joanie Stone

CANDLEWICK PRESS

*Dedicated to all the original Emily fans
and hopefully to a whole generation
of new ones. Swishy wishes!*
LK

*For Jenee—no one else I'd rather
be mermaids with.*
JS

Text copyright © 2022 by Liz Kessler
Illustrations copyright © 2022 by Joanie Stone

First edition 2022

Library of Congress Catalog Card Number 2021947070
ISBN 978-1-5362-1522-9 (hardcover)
ISBN 978-1-5362-2554-9 (paperback)

22 23 24 25 26 27 APS 10 9 8 7 6 5 4 3 2

Printed in Humen, Dongguan, China

This book was typeset in Stempel Schneidler.
The illustrations were created digitally.

Candlewick Press
99 Dover Street
Somerville, Massachusetts 02144

www.candlewick.com

CONTENTS

CHAPTER ONE
Swimming Lessons

It was a beautiful day in Brightport.

Emily Windsnap was sitting on the beach, making a sandcastle. But she really wanted to be playing in the ocean with the other kids.

"Please can I go in the water?" Emily
asked her mom.

"It's too dangerous," her mom said.
"You never know what's in the ocean."

Her mother always said no. So Emily had never learned to swim, even though they lived on a boat! But she wanted to so badly it hurt.

It would be OK if she had a friend to play on the beach with. But none of the other kids wanted to sit on the sand all day.

Emily looked out at the kids laughing
and splashing in the water and sighed. Then
she started another sandcastle.

A couple of weeks later, Emily's chance
finally came.

Her school was offering swimming
lessons. Finally Emily would learn how
to swim like the other kids! It would be
safe to learn at a pool, Emily thought.

And once she could swim, maybe her mom would let her go in the ocean!

When her class got to the pool, everyone changed into their bathing suits. Then they waited for the instructor.

But the water seemed to
be calling Emily.

She dipped a toe in.

Then she took a little step.

Then another.

She knew she should wait, but Emily
couldn't help it.

One more step.

And then—

Whoosh! She was underwater.

CHAPTER TWO
What's Happening?

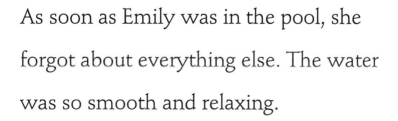

As soon as Emily was in the pool, she
forgot about everything else. The water
was so smooth and relaxing.

Then, wait . . . what was that?

Something was happening to her feet.
They weren't kicking anymore.

Then the weird feeling in her feet
climbed up her body, and her legs were
stuck together!

Emily came up for air and flapped her
arms, splashing water everywhere.

"Help!" she yelled.

The instructor dived in and carried Emily out of the water.

"You'll be fine," he said. "You just got a cramp."

He told Emily to sit beside the pool for the rest of the class. While she watched

everyone else swim, Emily thought about how she'd felt underwater. At first it was amazing, but then it was weird—and a little scary.

Emily tried to tell herself it was just a cramp, like the instructor said.

But he hadn't felt what Emily had felt. And it hadn't felt like a cramp.

Emily didn't know exactly what it was, but she knew something strange had happened when she tried to swim.

The even stranger thing was, she wanted to do it again.

CHAPTER THREE
Splash!

Emily couldn't sleep. She kept thinking about how she had felt in the pool.

Yes, she had been afraid. And no, she didn't know what had happened.

But when she thought about being in the water, it made her whole body tingle with excitement.

She knew she had to try it again.

She put on her bathing suit and crept out of her room.

A loud snore came from her mom's bedroom.

Before she could change her mind, she
sneaked out the door and tiptoed down
the dock to the beach.

She took a step into the waves.

Then another.

Then . . . *SPLASH!* She was in the water.

She dived under and stretched
her arms out.

And then it happened.

Again.

Her legs were stuck together! She
tried to kick, but nothing happened.

"Stay calm, stay calm," she said
to herself. "It's only a cramp."

But the cramp didn't go away. And soon Emily couldn't feel her feet at all.

She started to panic!

Emily looked down at her legs.

But she didn't have any feet. Then she
didn't have any legs.

Instead, she had a long, shiny,

beautiful tail!

CHAPTER FOUR
A Tail

Emily rubbed her eyes. She couldn't believe what she was seeing.

A tail? She had a tail?

She must be dreaming.

She pinched herself. Ouch! She was definitely awake.

Then she realized she was breathing underwater!

It didn't make sense.

It wasn't even possible.

But it was true.

She was a mermaid!

Emily swished and splished and swooshed and splashed. She'd never even been in the ocean before, and now she was swimming up, down, and around.

She stopped for a minute and
looked at the water all around her—
so huge and deep.

Then she looked down.

What was that on the seabed?

There was a dark shape beneath her.
She heard her mother's voice in her head:
It's too dangerous. It's not safe. It must be a
shark. It was coming for her! It would eat
her up!

Emily kicked her tail as hard as she
could.

She felt something touch her shoulder.
The shark had gotten her!

Then she heard a voice say, "It's OK. Come with me."

Emily spun around to see a girl reaching out to her.

"Come on," the girl said. "Grab my hand."

Together they swam away as fast
as they could.

CHAPTER FIVE
Rainbow Rocks

When they got to the surface, Emily
could see a group of rocks in the
moonlight.

"Where are we?" Emily asked.

"Rainbow Rocks. My favorite place," the girl replied.

"What's your name?"

"I'm Shona," said the girl.

"I'm Emily," said Emily. She realized the girl was flicking her tail back and forth under the water. "You're a mermaid!" Emily said.

"Of course," Shona said. "Aren't you?"

"Yes, I guess I am. But I only just found out tonight. Most of the time I'm a human."

Shona smiled. "That explains why I've never seen you before. Why are you out so late, though?"

"Something weird happened when I tried to swim in the pool, so I snuck out after my mom fell asleep to try to swim again. That's when I realized my legs turned into a tail!"

"I've always had my tail," said Shona.

"Are there lots of mermaids?" Emily asked.

"Of course!" said Shona. "We live in Shiprock. It's not too far from here."

"Why are you out here at night?" Emily asked.

"I couldn't sleep," said Shona. "So I decided to go for a swim. I thought I might practice my singing. But then I saw you instead!"

"Well, that was lucky for me! Thanks for saving me from that shark. I thought I was a goner for sure."

Shona laughed.

"That wasn't a shark," she said. "It was just some rocks and seaweed!"

Rocks and seaweed?

Before she knew it, Emily was laughing, too.

"Maybe you could help me figure this whole tail thing out?" Emily asked shyly.

"Sure!" said Shona, and she dived

deeper into the water. As she did, she

flicked her tail in the air. Then she spun

around in circles. She zoomed down to the
seabed and back up to the surface, then
twirled around and around.

Emily did her best to copy her. She was
only able to twirl in a few circles before she
got dizzy.

Both girls were smiling when they came back to the surface.

"Come on, let's go back to Rainbow

Rocks for a rest," Shona said.

They swam to the rocks together,

giggling and talking all the way.

CHAPTER SIX
Friendship Pebbles

Emily sat on the edge of a rock. "That was fun," she said.

"It was swishy!" Shona said.

Swishy? Emily liked that.

It was starting to get lighter out.

"I should probably go home before my mom wakes up," Emily said.

"Wait!" Shona slipped off the rock and dived into the water.

A moment later, she was back. She held out two shiny stones.

"Here," she said, handing one to Emily.

"What are they?" Emily asked.

"They're friendship pebbles. They mean we'll always be friends," Shona said.

Emily smiled. "Swishy!" she said.

"See you again soon?" Shona asked.

"Definitely!" Emily said.

And with a twirly, splish-splashy hug, the girls said goodbye.

Emily swam back to the beach. Once she was out of the water, her tail turned back into legs.

She ran to her boat and sneaked into bed just before her alarm went off.

*　*　*

Emily put her friendship pebble in her pocket as she left for school. All day she smiled to herself, thinking about her tail and her new friend and the fun they'd had.

And the best thing of all?

She had a feeling the adventures had only just begun!

The World of Emily Windsnap

Emily's Big Discovery

by Liz Kessler   illustrated by Joanie Stone

CANDLEWICK PRESS
www.candlewick.com